GWANGO'S
LONESOME
TRAIL

red
cygnet™
PRESS

*To Mom and Dad, for all those tent trailer trips we took
in the summertime of my youth. From Yellowstone Park to the
Devil's Tower, from Roswell to Vernal and everyplace in between,
thanks for showing a kid the grandeur and quirk of America.*

And to Claude Bell, father of the great dinosaurs of the Cabazon desert.

–J.P.

Illustrations copyright © 2007 Justin Parpan
Manuscript copyright © 2007 Justin Parpan
Book copyright © 2007 Red Cygnet Press, Inc., 11858 Stoney Peak Dr. #525, San Diego, CA 92128

Cover and book design: Amy Stirnkorb

First Edition 2007
10 9 8 7 6 5 4 3 2
Printed in China

Library of Congress Cataloging-in-Publication Data
is available at our website: www.redcygnet.com

GWANGO'S LONESOME TRAIL

WRITTEN AND ILLUSTRATED BY JUSTIN PARPAN

red
cygnet™
P R E S S

San Diego, California

The deserts of Santa Pocatello are a harsh and lonely place. The nearby town of sixty souls is little more than a pit stop for folks on their way to the vacation kingdom of California.

The people of this forgotten region tell a curious tale. It's quite a hum-dinger, about a prehistoric reptile said to wander the land of empty motels and sad cafés.

My name is Slim. I'll tell ya the story.

Weary truck drivers and gas station attendants called the creature Gwango. He was what you might call a rarity—one in a small handful of strange prehistoric reptiles that still roamed the wild regions of America.

Gwango was the loneliest of them all. Every day, he scoured the land for the company of a prehistoric "amigo" exactly like himself.

One dusty summer day, Gwango came upon a scaly little lizard baking in the hot sun.

"Holy mackerel!" said Gwango to himself. The lizard had skin as rough as sandpaper, just like Gwango. He was sure he had found the perfect amigo, and Gwango's laughter rocked the land like thunder!

But the little lizard was offended by Gwango's breath, which reeked of guacamole. In the blink of an eye, the lizard skittered away.

Gwango was embarrassed, and his laughter quickly ended. "Adiós," he whispered to the little lizard, as he thundered onward down his lonely trail.

As the wind kicked up, Gwango sniffed a smell—a breath as strong as his own.

Gwango tracked the odor to the top of a dune. There, he found a bear named Tartok, from the traveling circus.

"Holy moley!" cried Gwango, more excited than a kid on Christmas morning. This bear reeked of many great smells! He smelled of salty oysters, week-old enchiladas, and the greatest smell of all—guacamole!

Gwango's excitement caused his tail to wag from side to side. His tail was a mountainous thing, and all its wagging gave rise to the worst sandstorm in Santa Pocatello history.

When the dust finally settled, Gwango found himself all alone. Gwango whispered, "adiós," and continued on his lonely trail.

The howling and hollering of a shiny Santa Fe train brought Gwango to a cliff overlooking the tracks.

The train came quickly. "Hot dog!" said Gwango. He loved to howl and holler, just like the train! Gwango thought he had found an amigo exactly like himself. He could hardly hold back his excitement.

But the Santa Fe train rushed by as quickly as can be. Gwango's jolly grin melted away as fast as a popsicle on a red-tile roof. "Adiós," he whispered sadly, and he thundered onward along his lonely trail.

By now, the deserts of Santa Pocatello were hotter than a plate of jalapeño nachos. Gwango was tuckered out, so he stopped into a Polynesian motor hotel for a quick rest.

He was snacking on palm fronds when he came upon a Tiki statue lounging in the green Bermuda grass.

"Jiminy Christmas!" cried Gwango. The Tiki was big and bizarre, with a massive mouth full of teeth as long as brand-new pencils, just like Gwango's!

Then Gwango noticed something. A little human
being had already befriended the Tiki, and it looked
as if the two were having a grand old time.

Gwango let out a sad sigh that shook the palm trees
like a hurricane wind. He felt more alone than ever.
Slowly, he made his way back onto his lonely trail.

Gwango took his search for friendship into the barren hills of Santa Pocatello. To pass the time, he treated himself to a song about tumbleweeds, which he sang aloud.

His cheerful singing was cut short when he spotted something coming down the highway.

"Jumping Jehosephat!" cried Gwango. The approaching creature had the same brightly colored skin as him—flamingo pink with stripes of hot blue!

It was a family of happy campers on their way to Yellowstone Park. Gwango mistook their air-conditioned camper for a prehistoric reptile, so he chased them down the road.

The camper sped up and got away as Gwango's jolly grin disappeared. He stood quietly as the puttering engine drifted into silence. "Adiós," Gwango whispered sadly. Then he continued down his lonely trail.

The sun now dipped below the mountains, changing the light into quiet shadows. Gwango couldn't help but feel a little glum.

As he wandered through the valley of old prehistoric caves, Gwango stumbled upon a wondrous thing. It was big and strange, standing tall and fierce in the howling wind. It was brightly colored, and had skin like sandpaper.

It had a huge mouth, with long, sharp teeth. Best of all, it carried a potent stink that filled the air with a tremendous smell!

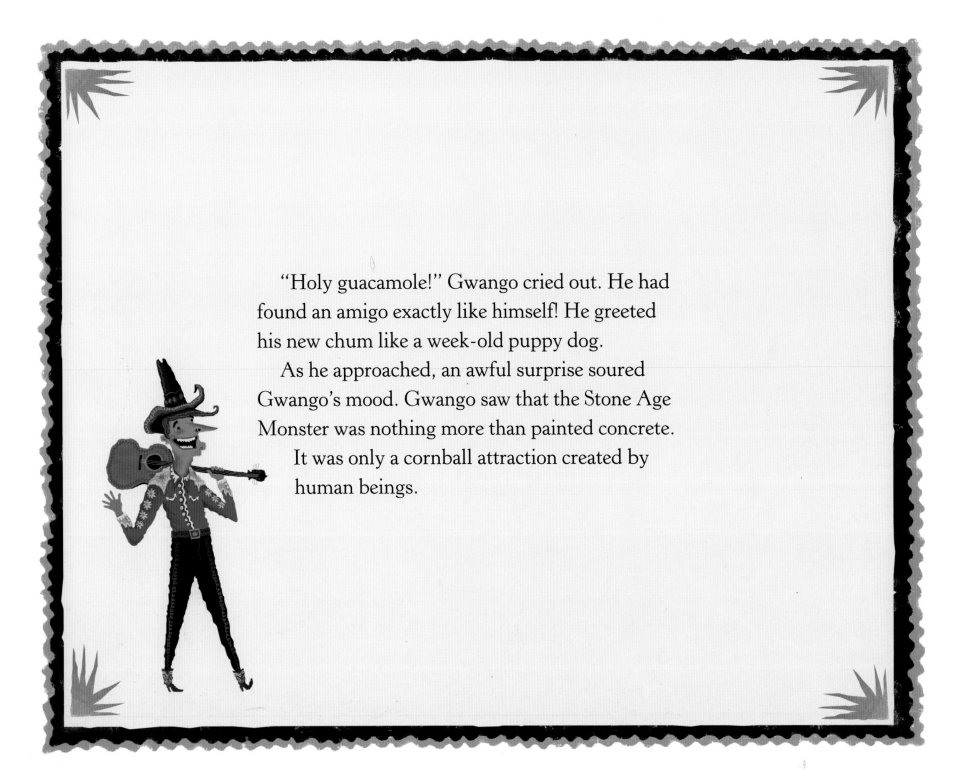

"Holy guacamole!" Gwango cried out. He had found an amigo exactly like himself! He greeted his new chum like a week-old puppy dog.

As he approached, an awful surprise soured Gwango's mood. Gwango saw that the Stone Age Monster was nothing more than painted concrete.

It was only a cornball attraction created by human beings.

Gwango knew he had finally come to the end of his trail.

He was feeling lonelier than a trucker on a midnight run. Then he had a thought. He decided to stop by the old drive-in movie theater to forget his troubles.

Sam was the drive-in's lonely projectionist. He was taking a popcorn break when he noticed Gwango watching a film about a man-eating dinosaur.

"Holy Toledo!" Sam cried out. He was absolutely thrilled. No one ever came to visit his old drive-in anymore!

Sam ran outside and watched the rest of the movie with Gwango. Together, they snickered at the terrible acting and the cheesy special effects.

When the movie was over, the two were laughing harder than they had ever laughed before. "You're a far-out fellow," Sam said to Gwango. "And I want you to know, you'll always have a friend here at the old drive-in."

Kindness like Sam's was a rare thing in the harsh desert, and it had a remarkable effect.

Gwango lit up inside. From head to tail, his towering form began to glow, more brilliant than any neon sign known to man.

It was a fantastic spectacle! From the desert twilight, the scattered people of Santa Pocatello followed the glow and came out to see.

"I want you to meet Gwango the Great!"
Sam the projectionist declared to the crowd.
"He's a one-of-a-kind fellow, and a true friend
to all the people of Santa Pocatello!"
The crowd let out a cheer. Gwango's light
had made everyone especially happy. Someone
suggested that a grand fiesta should be held
in Gwango's honor. Everyone agreed.

The fiesta lasted long into the night, until the early dawn brought the promise of a new day.

All the town's people drifted back to their little homes. Sam went to sleep in his projection room, and Gwango thundered onward, this time with a huge smile on his face.

For years to come, Gwango was a great beacon for all to see. And thanks to him, the deserts of Santa Pocatello never seemed lonely again.